A Perfectly MESSeD-UP Story

PATRICK McDONNELL

LITTLE, BROWN AND COMPANY
NEW YORK   BOSTON

Copyright © 2014 by Patrick McDonnell
Cover art © 2014 by Patrick McDonnell
Cover design by Jeff Schulz/Menagerie Co.
Cover copyright © 2014 Hachette Book Group, Inc.

Little, Brown and Company

Hachette Book Group
237 Park Avenue, New York, NY 10017
Visit our website at lb-kids.com

Little, Brown and Company is a division of Hachette Book Group, Inc.
The Little, Brown name and logo are trademarks of Hachette Book Group, Inc.

The publisher is not responsible for websites (or their content) that are not owned by the publisher.

First Edition: October 2014

Library of Congress Cataloging-in-Publication Data

McDonnell, Patrick, 1956– author, illustrator.
A perfectly messed-up story / by Patrick McDonnell. — First edition.
     pages cm
Summary: Louie becomes angry when the story in which he appears is ruined by messes from jelly,
peanut butter, and other things that do not belong in books.
ISBN 978-0-316-22258-7 (hardcover)
[1. Books and reading—Fiction.] I. Title.
PZ7.M1554Per 2014
[E]—dc23
                                   2013041668

10 9 8 7 6 5 4 3 2 1

SC

Printed in China

About This (Messed-Up) Book

This book was edited by Andrea Spooner and designed by Jeff Schulz and Patrick McDonnell with art direction by Patti Ann Harris. The production was
supervised by Erika Schwartz, and the production editor was Barbara Bakowski. The illustrations for this book were done in pen and ink, brush pen, crayon,
and watercolor on watercolor paper. Jeff Schulz takes responsibility for most of the messes. The text was set in Century Schoolbook and in a custom hand-
lettered font, and the display type is Century Schoolbook, with hand-lettered embellishments. No pages were harmed in the making of this book.

This is
Louie's story.

Once upon a time, little Louie
went skipping merrily along.

"Tra la la la la," he sang.

For in his heart,
Louie knew everything
was just

PLOP!

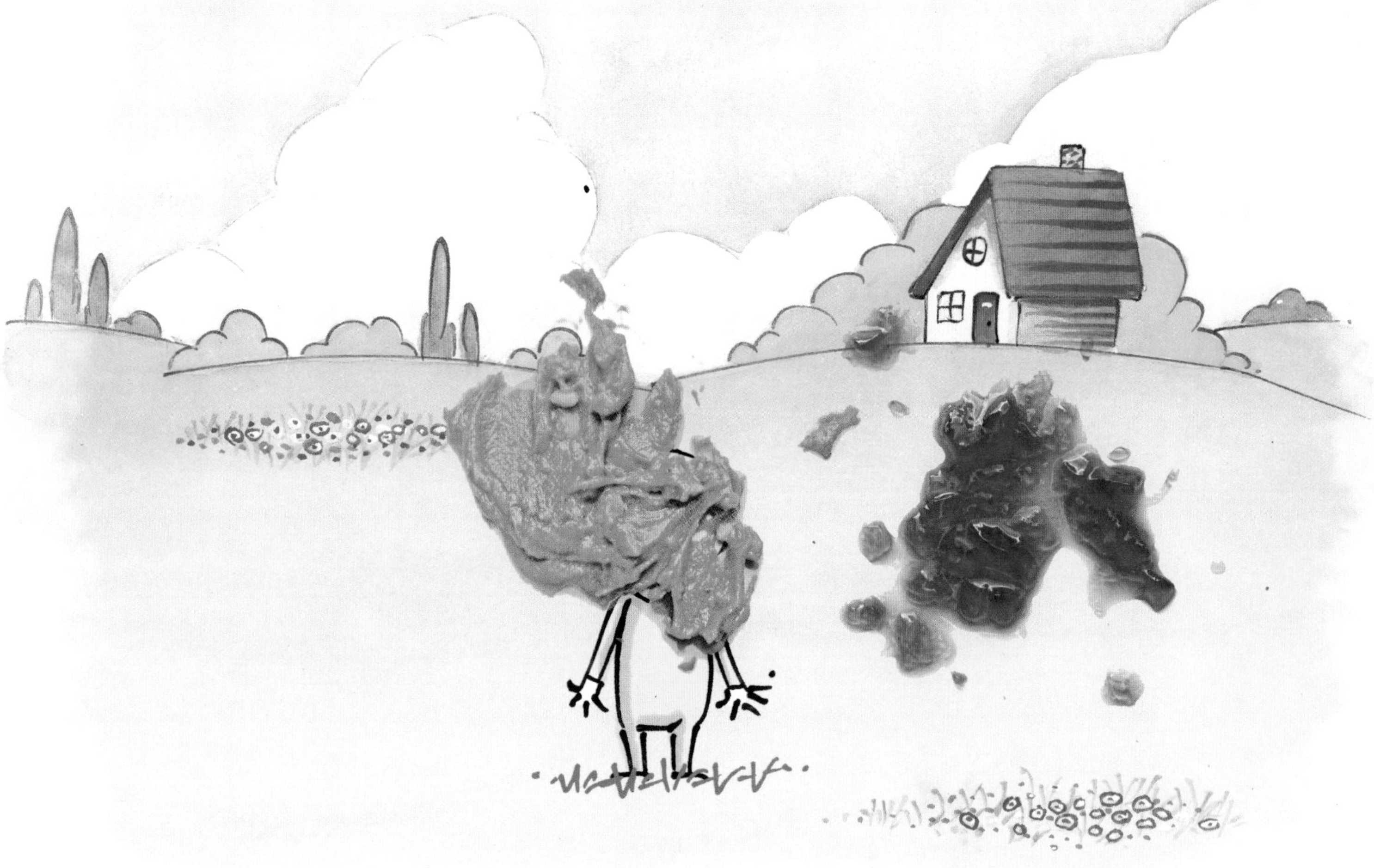

Once upon a time, little Louie
went skipping merrily along.

This is
Louie's story.

Once upon a time, little Louie
went skipping merrily along.
"Tra la la la la," he sang.

For in his heart,
Louie knew everything
was just...

This is
Louie's story.

The
End